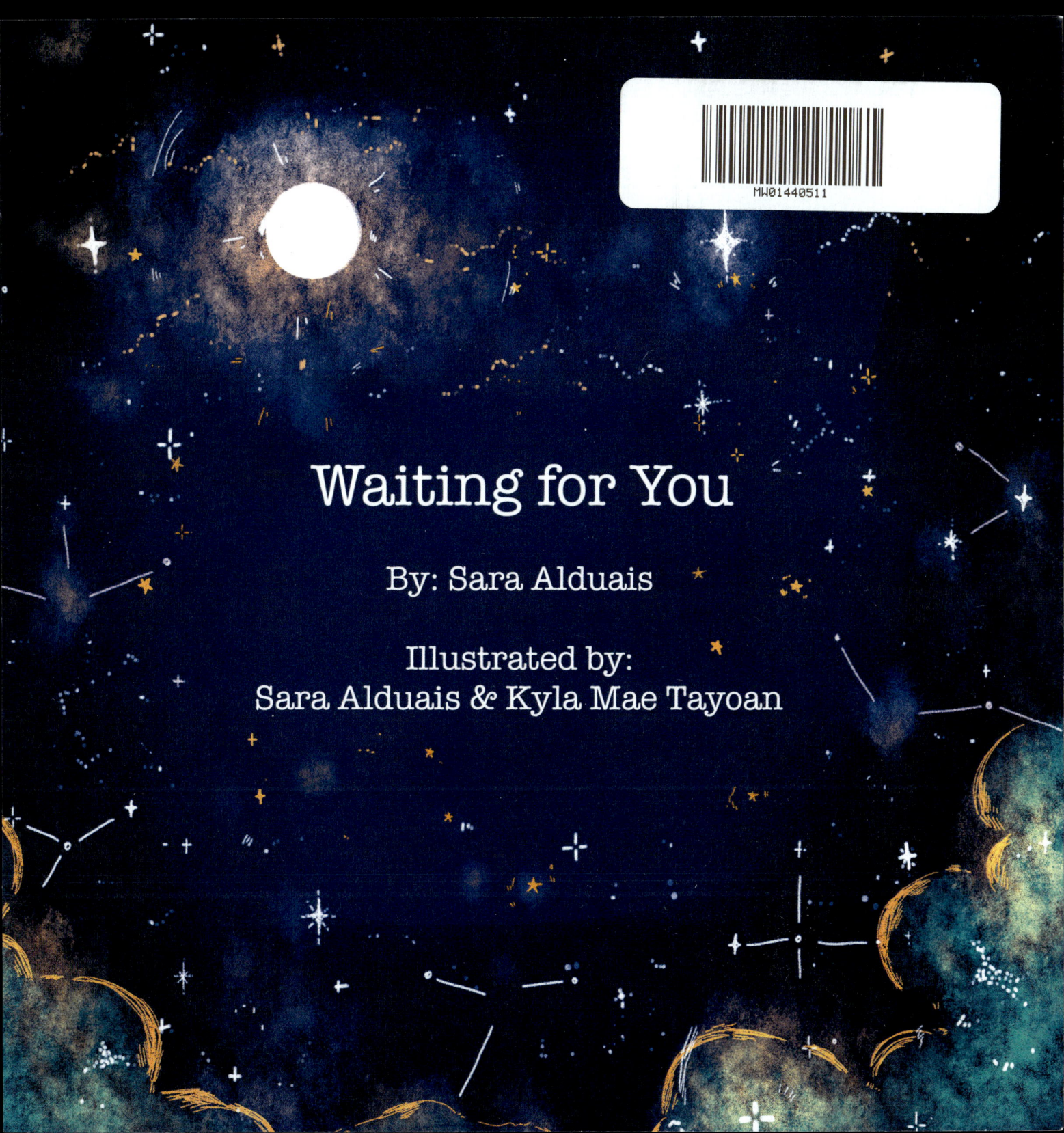

# Waiting for You

By: Sara Alduais

Illustrated by:
Sara Alduais & Kyla Mae Tayoan

Waiting For You by Sara Alduais

Published through Amazon KDP

Copyright © 2022 Sara Alduais.

All rights reserved. This book or any portion thereof may not be reproduced or used in any manner whatsoever without the express written permission of the publisher except for the use of brief quotations in a book review and as permitted by U.S. copyright law.

Cover and Illustrations by Sara Alduais and Kyla Mae Tayoan

ISBN: 9798443931388

Printed in the United States of America

dedicated to, my moon

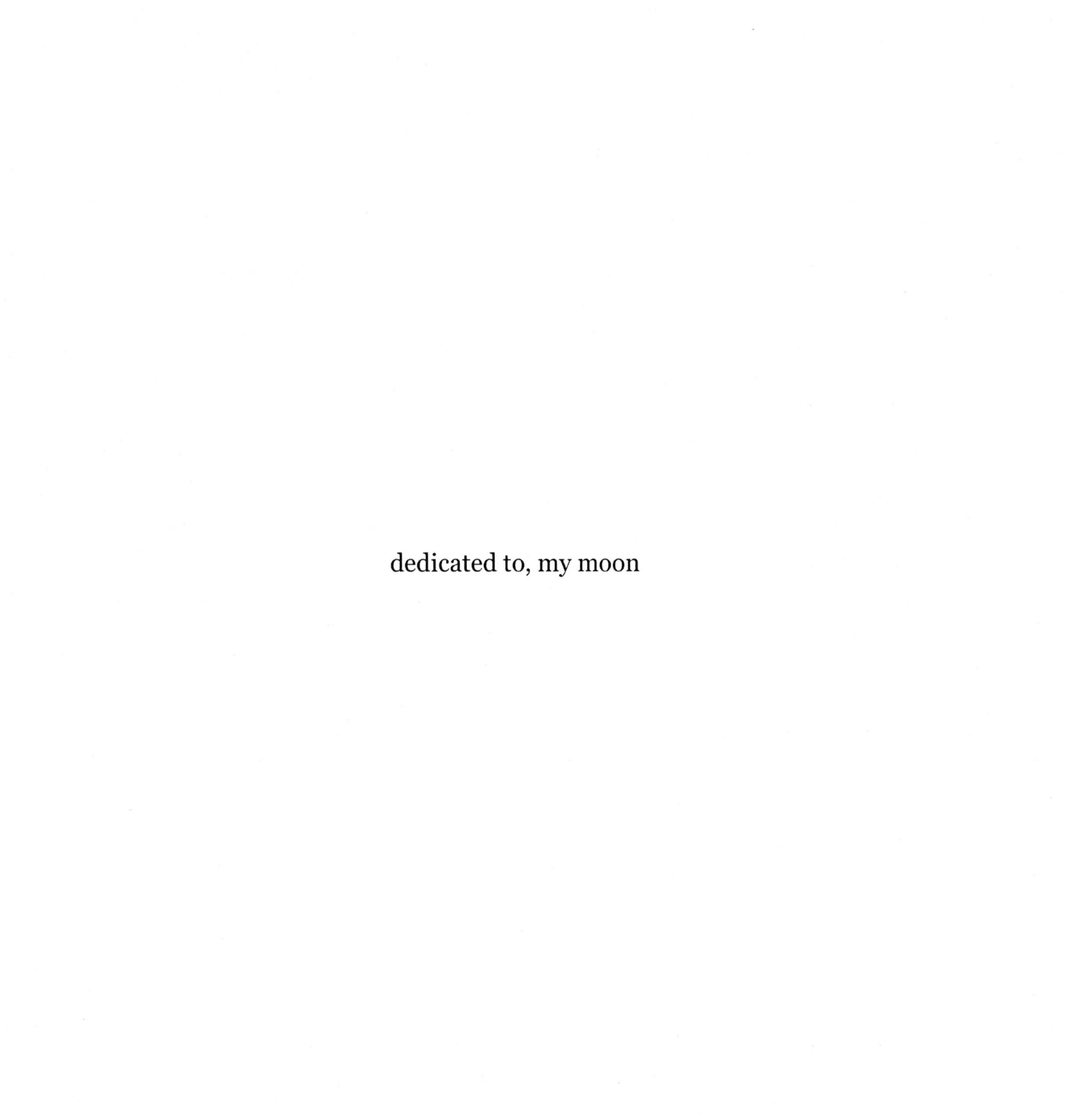

I found a friend in the moon, and a friend in myself
- C.S

The sky is dark, the stars are high,
the soft moon illuminates the sky.

Sofia can't sleep, so she leaves her room. She goes to get help from her friend the moon.

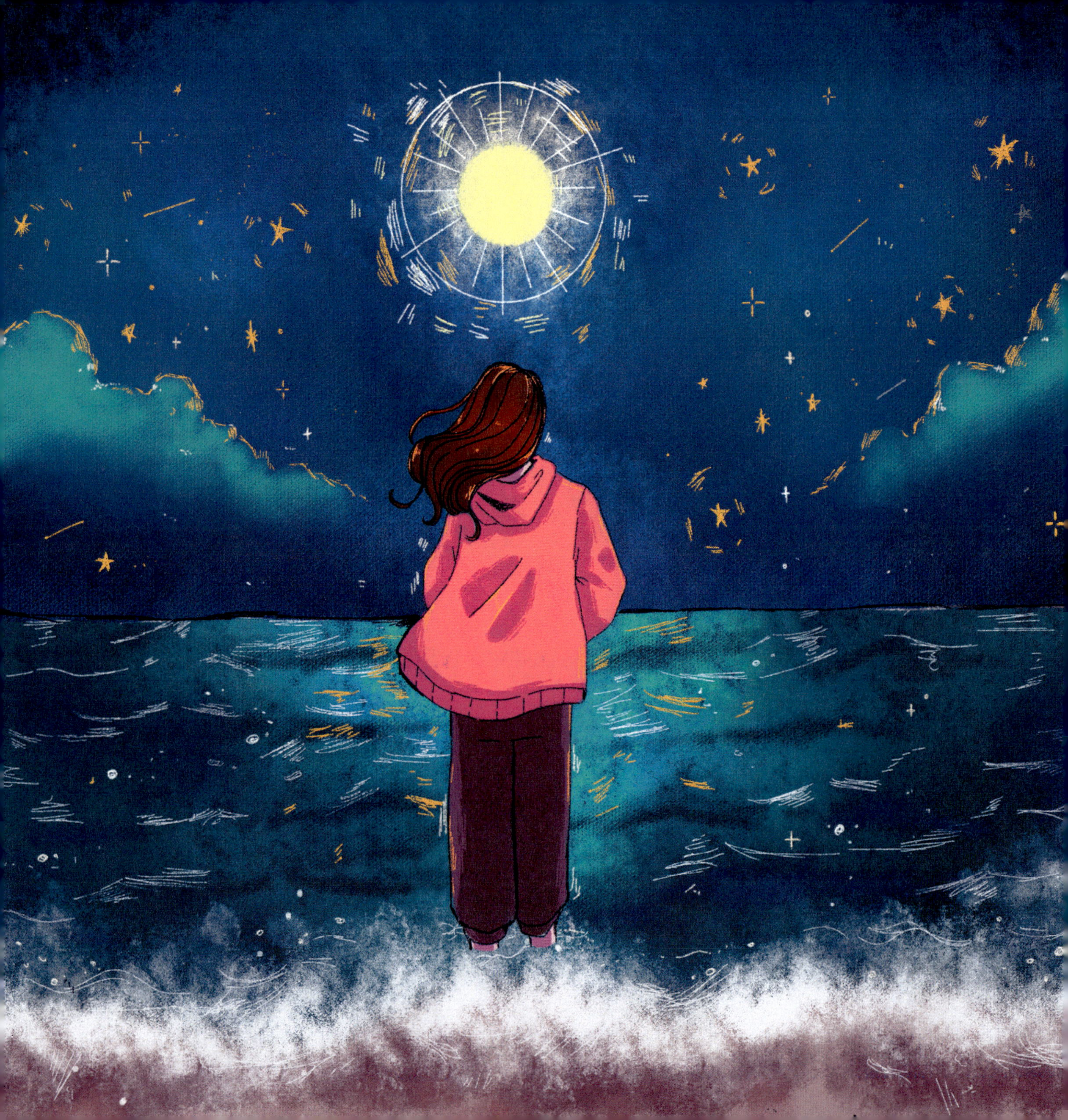

Sofia talks to her friend and tells him about her day. But the moon never has a thing to say.

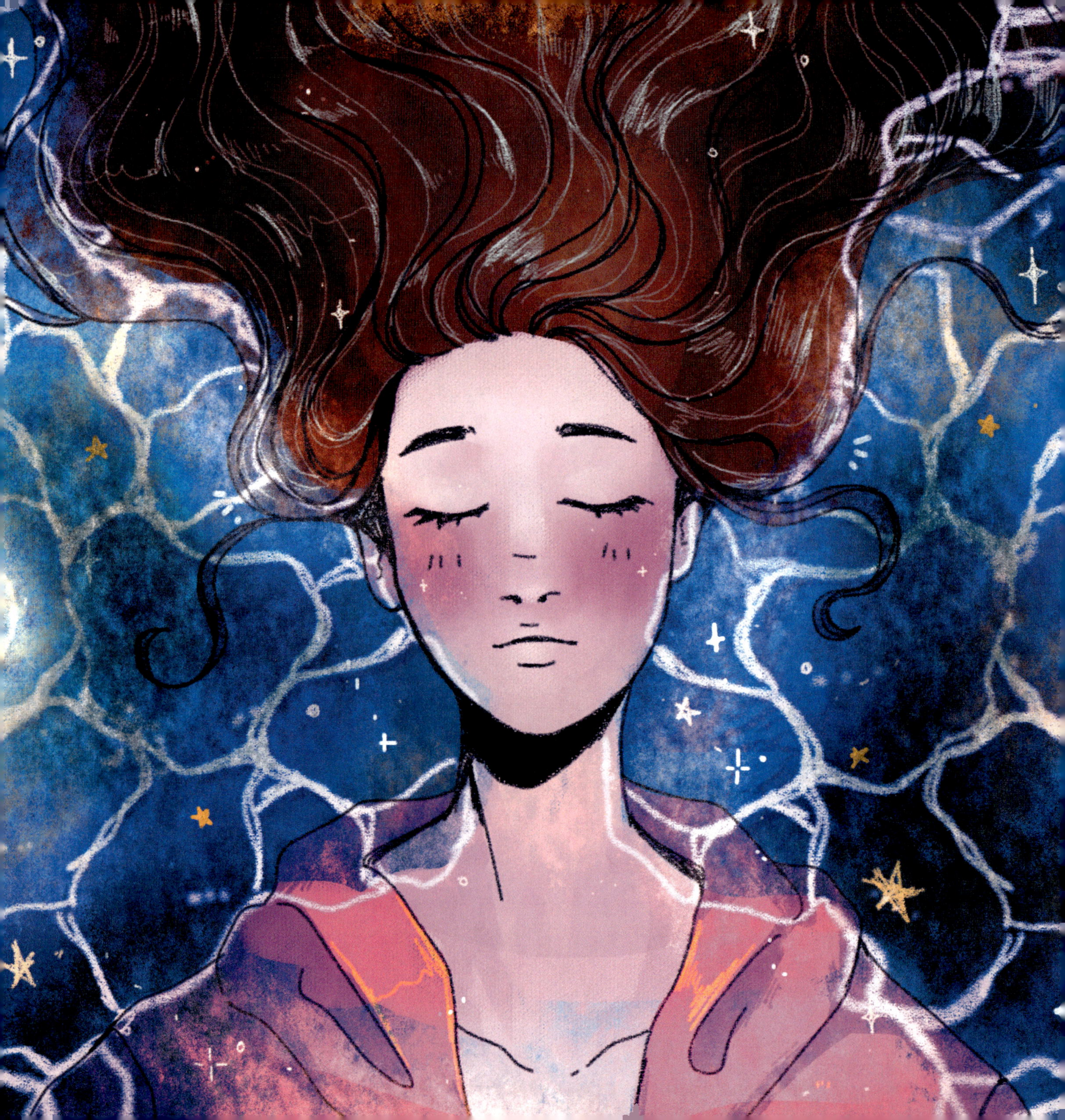

Sofia decides to go for a swim, to calm
her down and let the sleep wash in.

She lays on her back and closes her eyes,
something magical happens, she begins to fly!
Her clothes transform, a dress pretty and white,
as she spins and twirls into the night.

The moon begins to laugh as her feet wobble and kick, it says, "What are you doing, my friend?" with a voice beautiful and rich.

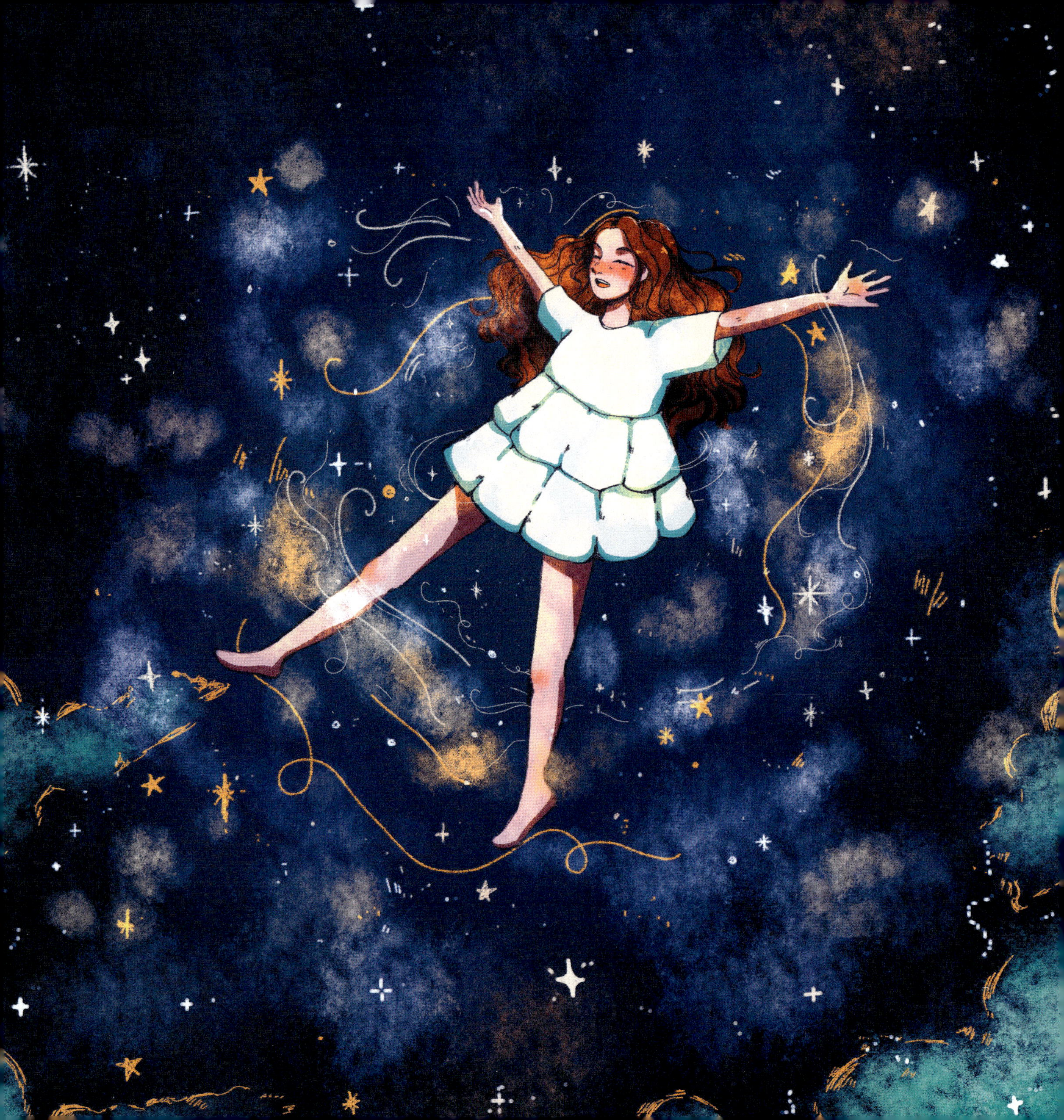

"I'm flying!" She shouts her heart full and new.
"Did you make me fly, Moon?"
"No friend, this was inside of you."

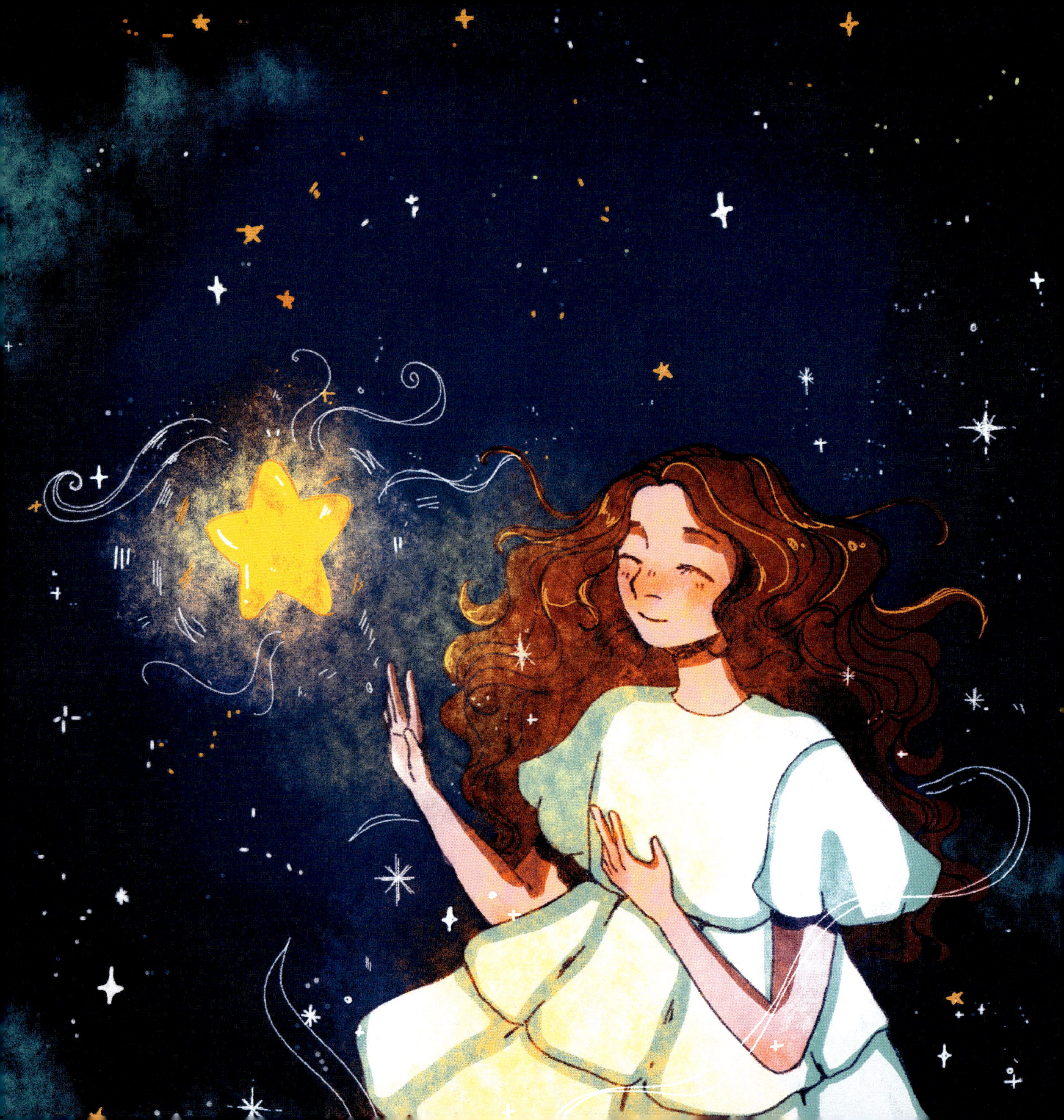

Just then a little star wiggles and soars, together they race and float above the shores.

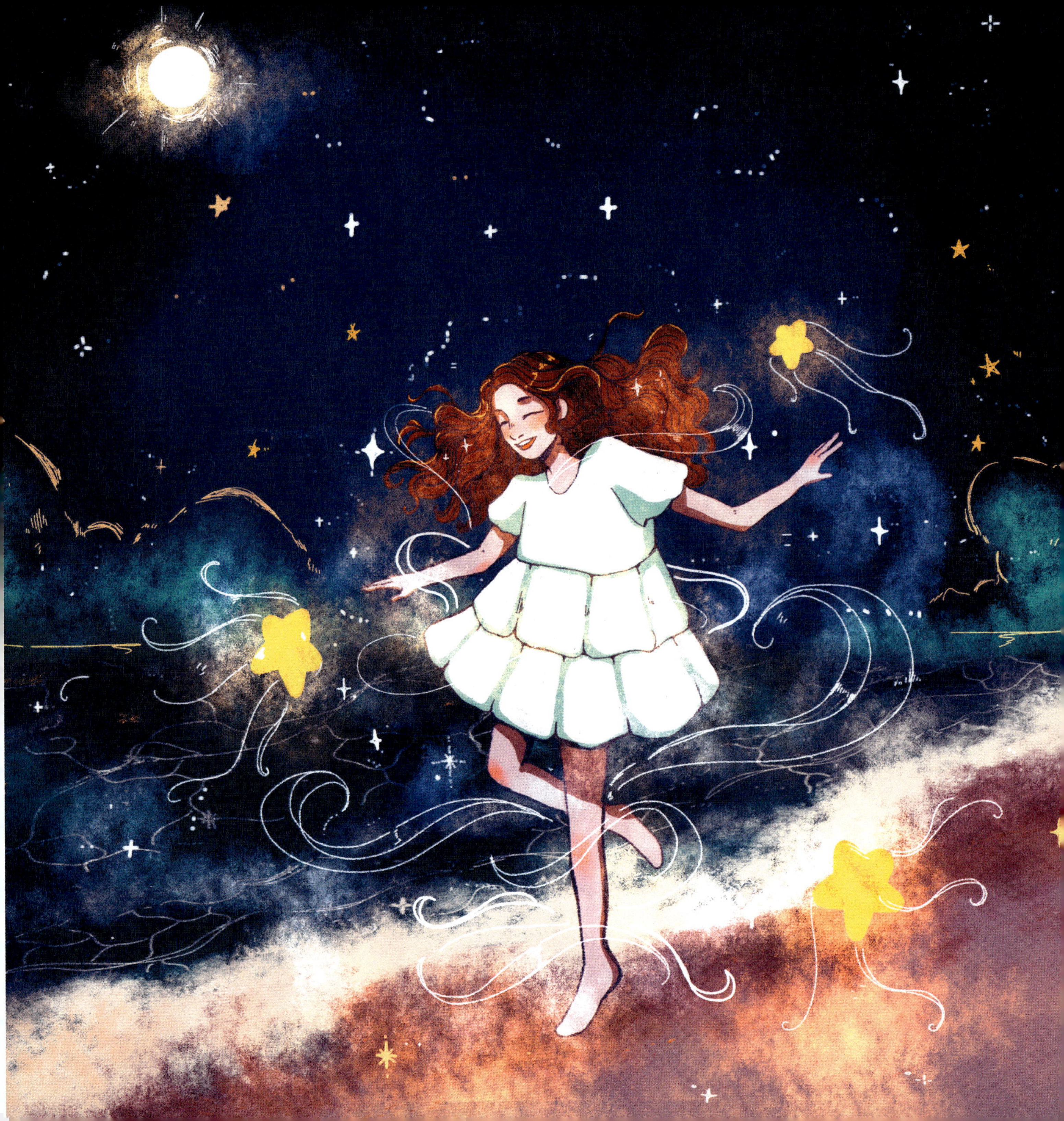

Sofia plays with her friends, flying through the sky, she has so much fun she never wants to say goodbye.

The moon calls to Sofia to land back on the beach, "Friend, it's time for us to go, and tomorrow we will meet."

"No!" Sofia cries, "I don't want you to leave. I want to stay here with the Stars, pretty pretty please?" "I'm sorry my friend the Sun is coming soon. I'll be back tomorrow; I promise I'm still your Moon"

Stars rush to Sofia, a hug before they're gone. The moon says softly "Would you like me to sing a song?"

*Shining bright in the sky*
*Like the tide hits the shore*
*I am yours, and you are mine*
*I will come back each night*
*We will fly among the stars*
*And I'll be waiting for you*
*Forever in your heart*

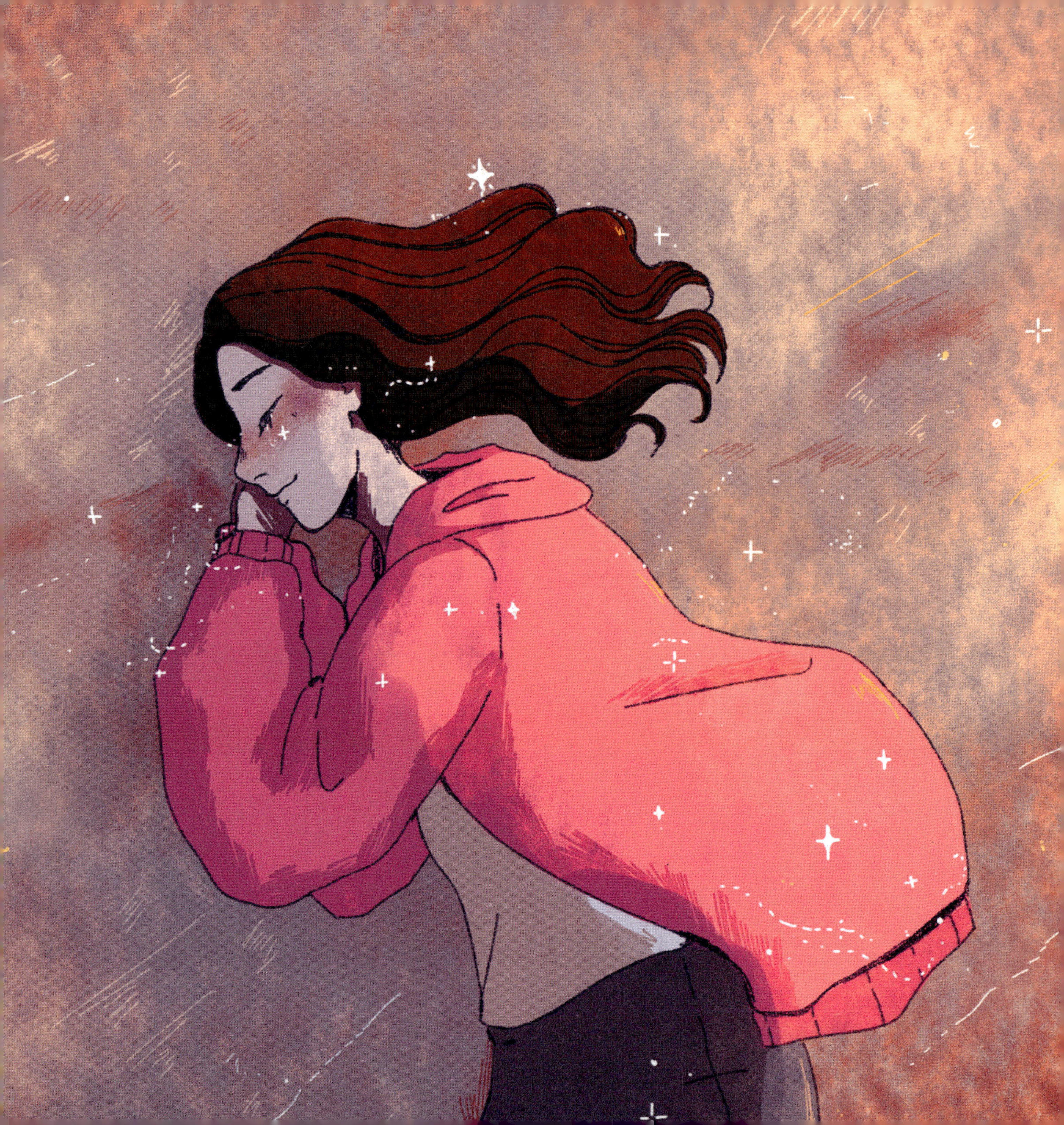

Sofia lays down and closes her eyes.
She has always hated goodbyes.
Sofia knows she will miss her friends, but
she will sleep and dream of them again.

Authors Note

This book has been one of the best and most frustrating things I've done so far in my life. It started off as a story I told my baby brother Ibrahim, the inspiration behind it all, to a contest entry that won first place, and finally built itself up into one of my greatest projects.
But I did not do this alone of course.

My own Stars who've helped me on this journey and made this book possible;
Mama and Baba
Kyla Mae
Amat and Khadeeja
Amal and Ahlam
Salwa Mawari

and the Moon behind it all
my aunt, Aisha

Thank you all for your support, guidance, and encouragement.

Made in the USA
Columbia, SC
08 September 2022